THE FABULOUS Song

For my brother David, who still plays
D.G.

To Gabriel, my favourite trumpet player
M.-L.G.

To Luka, Mia and Toby,
your accordion lessons start next week!
M.C. & D.G.

When Sarah Pipkin's brother was born,
they named him Frederic.

"As in Frederic Chopin," Mr. Pipkin announced,
"the great composer."

"Chopin was a genius,"
Mrs. Pipkin often added.

When the Pipkins took Frederic for walks
in his stroller, people always looked at him
and said, "My, what a beautiful baby."
"And musical, too," his mother would say.

Actually, Frederic wasn't a beautiful baby.
He looked like a turnip left too long on the windowsill.
He was wrinkled and pale, with a tuft of carrot-coloured hair.
He gurgled and made noises when he ate.

To Sarah it sounded like air leaking out
of a balloon, but to Mr. and Mrs. Pipkin
it sounded like a symphony.

When Frederic was five,
his parents gave him piano lessons
because Sarah had taken them.
The teacher's name was Mr. Stricter.
He lived in a dark house
and had a dog named Peanut
that barked at everything.

Frederic didn't like the piano.
What was worse, the piano didn't like Frederic.
When he played, it sounded like a brick
crashing through a window.

Allegro vivace

Presto

"I don't want to play the piano,"
he told his mother.
"You'll be glad you took lessons
when you grow up," she said.
"Then I don't want to grow up,"
Frederic replied.

After three months, Mr. Stricter told the Pipkins
that Frederic would never learn to play the piano.
They bought him a clarinet.

Frederic and Mrs. Pipkin took a bus
to the clarinet teacher's house.
Her name was Mrs. Lumply.
Frederic thought she looked
like a goldfish. When Frederic
blew into his clarinet,
it gave him a headache.

"You have to feel the music,"
Mrs. Lumply told Frederic.
The only thing he could feel
was the headache.

The best thing about the clarinet was that it was small enough
to leave on the bus, which Frederic did.
When they got home, his mother noticed the clarinet was missing.
"I must have left it on the bus," Frederic said. "By accident."
Mrs. Pipkin phoned the bus company.

The next day, Frederic and his mother drove to a warehouse
that was full of all the things people leave on buses.
There were sixteen clarinets, nine oboes, six saxophones,
eleven cellos, twenty-nine recorders and more than
a hundred violins. Frederic saw lots of other mothers
with children searching for lost instruments.
Mrs. Pipkin picked out Frederic's clarinet
and they went home.

Over the next few months, Frederic tried almost every instrument in the orchestra. The oboe sounded like a sick dog whining. The violin sounded like two cats fighting. He tried the saxophone, xylophone and trombone. When he blew into the trumpet, it sounded like a frog trying to spit. The banjo sounded like a frying pan hitting a frozen fence post. The cello sounded like an argument between four snakes.

Mrs. Pipkin gave Frederic a flute and stared at him hopefully. He blew into it, but no sound came out at all. Frederic went upstairs and played with his dinosaurs.

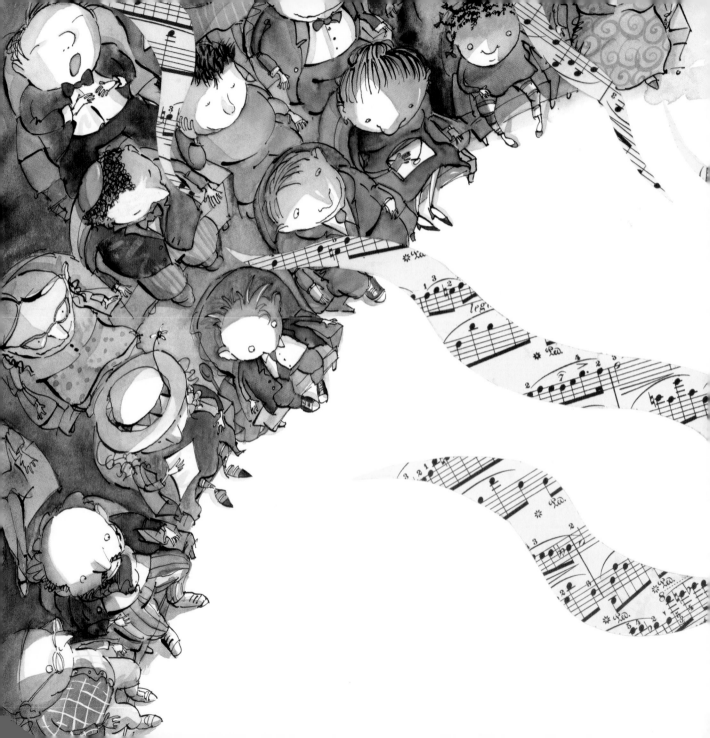

That evening, Frederic went to a concert with his parents.
Sarah was playing the piano in the youth orchestra.
Frederic squirmed in his chair until the conductor
tapped his baton three times and the orchestra
looked up at him, waiting. With one wave
of the baton, the orchestra began
to play. The baton leapt and swirled
through the air and the music leapt
and swirled with it. The conductor's
hair shook as he moved,
guiding the musicians.
He never made a sound,
but to Frederic he was amazing.

After the concert, everyone
congratulated Sarah on her piano playing.
"You were wonderful," his mother said.
"Really great," her father said.
"You have a pimple on your nose,"
Frederic said.
"Everyone was talking about it."

On Frederic's seventh birthday, the whole Pipkin family
gathered for a huge party. Uncles and aunts and cousins
and grandparents came to Frederic's house, and each one
brought a musical instrument. The house was full of musical Pipkins,
so full that no one could move.

The problem was, they all wanted to play a different song.
Grandpa Pipkin wanted "Happy Birthday," Grandma Pipkin wanted
"Michael Row the Boat Ashore" and two cousins began to play
"Old MacDonald Had a Farm." Sarah was tinkling away at the piano
and Frederic's aunt tooted "Jeepers Creepers" on her flute.

It was more like a herd of buffalo arguing
about the weather than a birthday party.

Frederic had to do something. He climbed up on a chair
and took his wooden spoon out of his pocket. He rapped it three times
on his uncle's head. His uncle shouted. The room became silent
as everyone stared up at Frederic in surprise.

Frederic waved the wooden spoon slowly.
With his other hand, he pointed
at his uncle, who began to plunk softly
on his banjo. It was a song that no one
had ever heard before; not even
his uncle knew what he was playing.

Frederic went on waving his spoon and the oboe
and guitar joined in. Then he nodded at the
violin and trumpet. Soon everyone was playing
the fabulous new song
and wondering where it had come from.

Frederic shook his hair
and thrashed his spoon
through the air
and the musical Pipkins shook
and thrashed along with him.
They played until
their faces were red,
until their arms were tired,
until their hearts were pounding.
They would have continued,
but Frederic lost his grip
on the wooden spoon
and it flew across the room.

The fabulous song ended
and no one knew where
it had come from
or where it had gone.

They were still wondering as they sat down at the table.
By the time dinner was served, they were arguing.
When dessert was carried in, they were all trying to hum
and whistle and sing the fabulous song.
It sounded like twelve rocket scientists talking backwards.

But Frederic wasn't listening. He had found his wooden spoon
behind the curtains and was eating his ice cream with it.
As he ate, he hummed quietly to himself. A new song,
a stupendous song, was playing in his head.

After dinner, the Pipkin Family Orchestra
would play it.
And he, the Great Frederic Pipkin,
would lead them.

Let Me Hear You Say

Lyrics Michelle Campagne and Don Gillmor → Music Michelle Campagne
Performance Michelle Campagne

This is my fabulous song
It's my fabulous song
It is a song that can be sung by anybody
This is my fabulous song
It's my fabulous song
And I want it to be sung by everybody
Well, it hasn't much to say
But I like it fine that way
So let me hear you say
It's a fabulous song

Every boy and every girl
Can sing together
I'd be so pleased if we
Could sing in perfect harmony

We'd sing this fabulous song
A fabulous song
It is a song that can be sung by anybody
Well, it hasn't much to say
But I like it fine that way
So let me hear you say
It's a fabulous song

Crazy for the Dinosaur

Lyrics Michelle Campagne and Don Gillmor → Music Michelle Campagne
Performance Harry Manx

I got a thing for dinosaurs
Well, I got lots and I want more
I got dinos everywhere
Well, I even have some on my underwear!

Because I'm crazy for the dinosaur

I know every dino known to man
Can you name them all?
Hey, I can!
Dino names impress the chicks
Like Thecodontosaurus and Sinosauropterix

Because they're crazy for the dinosaur

If I had a real dinosaur
I'd come knocking at your door
We could go play hide and seek
You know, Tyrannosaurus Rex is really very sweet

Dinosaur man, I love you
I'm crazy for you, man
Tyrannosaurus Rex, you rock!

Sarah's Brother
Lyrics **Michelle Campagne** and **Don Gillmor** → Music **Davy Gallant**
Performance **Deb Hay**

What's so great about my brother
All he does is sleep and cry
People say he's such a beauty
I can't help but wonder why
'Cause he's nothing much to look at
The word homely fits the bill
Like a turnip that's been left too long
On mother's window sill

Oh! Frederic
With your shocking hair of red
Wish you'd been a girl instead
Oh! Frederic
Can't you see you've got to go?
A little birdie told me so
Oh! Frederic

Frederic, like the composer
Is the silly name they gave
My guess is that Mr. Chopin
Is now turning in his grave
'Cause you gurgle, spill and spit
Sounds like a real cacophony
But my mother and my father
They just hear a symphony

Frederic
With your shocking hair of red
Wish you'd been a girl instead
Oh! Frederic
Can't you see you've got to go?
A little birdie told me so
Oh! Frederic

Mr. Stricter
Lyrics **Michelle Campagne** and **Don Gillmor** → Music **Davy Gallant**
Performance **David Francis**

It is written do re mi
And yet he plays a mi re do
When I should hear fa so la
My ears detect a la fa so
I just do not understand it
For the child is far from dim
Clearly Frederic does not like the piano
Nor does it like him

When assigned to my tutelage
Here's Stricter's rule of thumb:
If you cannot learn your lessons
You'll have none!

It is clear, I say, "Allegro"
And he plunks down listlessly
His pianissimo is forte
He crescendos aimlessly
And his tempo is atrocious
I don't wish to be unkind
But if the Pipkin boy keeps coming here
Then I shall lose my mind!

I must say, the boy is hopeless
He will never learn to play
And it frays my weary nerves
No, I cannot go on this way
I'm afraid for my dog Peanut
Such a sensitive canine
The music takes a toll on him
He has one life - not nine!

Mrs. Lumply's Goldfish

Lyrics **Michelle Campagne** and **Don Gillmor** → Music **Michelle Campagne** and **Davy Gallant**
Performance **Lorne Elliott**

One little fishy
Playing on her clarinet
You got to feel the music
Feel the music
Can you feel it?
"No!"
Well, then blow fish, blow fish, blow
Little fishy
Then blow fish, blow fish, blow!

Two little fishies
Playing on their clarinets
You got to feel the music
Gotta feel the music
Can you feel it?
"No!"
Then blow fish, blow fish, blow
Little fishies
Then blow fish, blow fish, blow!

Three little fishies
Playing on their clarinets
You got to feel the music
Feel the music
Can you feel it?
"No!"
"All I feel is the pounding of my head"
They said
"All I feel is the pounding of my head"

"Oh!"
Then go fish, go fish
Go little fishies
Then go fish, go fish, go!

By Accident on the Bus

Lyrics **Michelle Campagne** and **Don Gillmor** → Music **Davy Gallant**
Performance **Davy Gallant** with **Gabriel Campagne** and **Aleksi Campagne**

I forgot it on the bus
I didn't mean to
I forgot it on the bus
Oh! What a shame, such a shame
I forgot it on the bus
It was an accident
I forgot it on the bus
I'm going to miss it just the same

"People always forget things on buses"
"Really?"
"Yeah, it happens all the time"

My friend Jimmy left his homework
Uncle Tom left his umbrella
Dad forgot his purple mittens
That he got from Aunty Stella
Everyone's forgotten something
Sometime in their lives, I'll bet
So who could really blame me
If I left my clarinet?

"Oh man, your clarinet? The black one with the...
The shiny... things on it?"
"Yeah, that one. I was really broken up about it"

But there's a warehouse full of items
Other people leave behind
There are saxophones, recorders
Instruments of every kind
There are tubas, drums and trumpets
See, I'm not the only one
There are a hundred violins!
Oh yeah, and one accordion

"Just one?"
"Yeah, oddly enough, just one"
"Hmm"

I forgot it on the bus
I didn't mean to
I forgot it on the bus
Oh! What a shame, such a shame
I forgot it on the bus
It was an accident
I forgot it on the bus
But mother found it just the same

Dogs, Cats, Frogs, Frying Pans and Snakes

Lyrics **Michelle Campagne** and **Don Gillmor** → Music **Michelle Campagne** and **Davy Gallant**
Performance **Davy Gallant**

Dogs, cats, frogs
Frying pans and snakes

Four snakes sitting in the sun
Had an argument one day
Just as Frederic Pipkin's cello
Was about to play
It wasn't nice, it wasn't pretty
Frankly, it was kind of silly
When they all began to hiss
It sounded something like this

The first snake said to the second,
"You've got a funny looking tail
It's bent and crooked
Makes me laugh, it makes me wail!
Hey, hey, hey, hey!"
"How can you talk to me that way?
That's not a very nice thing to say!
We snakes should cherish one another
Like a sister, like a brother!"

"Words can hurt" the third chimed in
"Like sticks and stones on slimy skin
Our friend may shed a tear or two
I'd shed my skin if I were you!"
The fourth snake said, "To me it seems
You're like three slithering drama queens
Now just sit back, enjoy the sun
Hey, playing cello is really fun!"

As they hissed and sputtered, because snakes can
Like bacon in a frying pan
Frederic Pipkin struck the bow
On that unfortunate cello
I saw it all, yeah I was there
The cello gleamed in the sun's glare
The dogs and cats and frogs agreed
Snakes are one strange and crazy breed

Well I try and I try
But I just can't seem to get it
But you know I just won't let it
Get me down

The Amazing Conductor

Lyrics **Michelle Campagne** and **Don Gillmor** → Music **Michelle Campagne**
Performance **Michelle Campagne**

Bow tie, tux and tails
Striped pants and pointy shoes
He taps his baton
Strikes a pose and no one moves

Not a word, not a sound
Not one floutist's peep
Until his hand guides them all
The shepherd leads his trusting sheep

Into the music, which leaps and swirls
As does his baton
The conductor is amazing
This guy's got it going on

His hair shakes as he moves
As the music reached its peak
It was so beautiful
That a tear ran down my cheek
He orchestrated everything
And didn't even speak

Sarah Pipkin's Pimple

Lyrics **Michelle Campagne** and **Don Gillmor** → Music **Michelle Campagne**
Performance **Connie Kaldor**

The recital was just lovely
Everyone in town was there
There were bow ties, there were crinolines
And music in the air
And the orchestra was brilliant
And the thing that stole the show
Was the bloated round protrusion
On a little Pipkin nose

Have you seen it?
Have you set your eyes upon it?
It is hideously bulbous
No it's not a pretty dimple
Have you seen it?
It is really quite amazing
Have you spotted little Sarah Pipkin's pimple?

"It won't last," her mother said
"I want it gone now!" Sarah hissed
So they made a quick appointment
With a dermatologist
As the doctor poked and prodded saying,
"What do we have here?"
"Well," the pimple simply stated,
"I'm a zit. That much is clear"

It could talk! It was prodigious
And its face was kind of cute
And its views on global issues
Were astoundingly astute
So the TV crews descended
People came from miles around
And the pustulent protuberance
Soon became world renowned

But not everybody loved it
"It's grotesque" some did say
It simply stated, "You would not say that
Had you been born this way"
But its words were so enlightening
And they were noted quote for quote
Then one day, it simply vanished
And it left a farewell note

Adieu, adieu, my dear admirers
You've been great, you've filled my cup
But there's a time and place for everything
And well, my time is up
But I hope you've learned a lesson
From this small tumescent mound
That in every living creature
There is beauty to be found

Had you seen it?
Had you set your eyes upon it?
It was clever, it sang showtunes
And its message was so simple
Had you seen it?
It was really quite amazing
We will never forget Sarah Pipkin's pimple

Frederic's Wooden Spoon

Lyrics **Michelle Campagne** and **Don Gillmor** → Music **Michelle Campagne**
Adapted from **Chopin's "Waltz 1"** → Performance **Michael Burgess**

Frederic's wooden spoon
Was a magical thing
Frederic's wooden spoon

Frederic's wooden spoon
Oh, the magic you see
Comes from the tree
From whence it came

Oh, it followed him everywhere Frederic went
Back pocket or pack sack, its handle was bent
But he loved and admired that big wooden spoon
Every night in his bed by the light of the moon

Yes, the wooden spoon had a fine story to tell
Of forests in Holland where many birds dwell
You see, Chopin himself wrote a piece in the shade
Of the tree from which Frederic's spoon was made

Tweet tweet... tweet tweet...
Was the song Chopin heard
Sung by a bird
Perched right above him
Tweet tweet... tweet tweet...
In the shade of a tree
From which would be
Made Frederic's spoon

The Birthday Party

Lyrics **Michelle Campagne** and **Don Gillmor** → Music **Michelle Campagne** and **Davy Gallant**
Performance **Michelle Campagne** and **Davy Gallant**

The Fabulous Song

Lyrics **Michelle Campagne** and **Don Gillmor** → Music **Michelle Campagne**
Performance **Daniel Lavoie**

This is my fabulous song...

We begin with the banjo
Plunking soft and steady
Then the oboe comes in
With a sweet simple melody
The guitar strums in rhythm
Is the harmony ready?
Now trumpet, you blow
Violin, strike the bow

Oh, this is my fabulous song

If you follow me, you won't go wrong
Bluejays and chickadees
Flutter outside my window
To and fro
Like a violin bow

Oh, this is my fabulous song

Beautiful music awaits in my heart
That's where it starts
And it flows out of my hands
Into the magical world
Of melody, harmony and rhythm
And then I've written
This fabulous song

When you find something
That touches your soul
Makes you feel whole
Then you discover that dreams
They really do come true
Your future is hopeful and bright
And you can write
Your own fabulous song

If you dare to follow me
Then my friend, just wait and see
We will make sounds so pleasing
Blow the reed, strike up the bow
You will feel the music flow
Just come this way and play
My fabulous song

Story **Don Gillmor** → Illustrations **Marie-Louise Gay** → Songs **Michelle Campagne**
and **Davy Gallant** → Record Producer **Davy Gallant** → Artistic Director **Roland Stringer**
Graphic Design **Stephan Lorti** → Recorded, mixed and mastered by **Davy Gallant**
assisted by **Pascal Theriault** at **Dogger Pond Studio**
Additional recording by **Nik Tjelios** at **Casa Wroxton Studio**

www.thesecretmountain.com
℗ 2005 **Folle Avoine Productions** → © 2005 **Lac Laplume Music** → ISBN 2-923163-17-6

We acknowledge the financial support of the Government of Canada
through the Canada Music Fund for this project

First printed in Hong Kong, China by Book Art Inc., Toronto